This Book Belongs To

_____

WHEN PIG GOT STUCK IN THE TROUGH

Written by Dave Thorne

Illustrated by Kris Lillyman

Of all of the pigs that lived in the sty
The one they call Dougie will sure catch your eye
He's like all the rest as he's pink and he's grubby
But compared to the rest he's exceptionally chubby

Dougie the piggy's a hungry old soul
He eats much too fast - eating everything whole
He doesn't have manners. He just doesn't share
And greedy old Dougie – well - just doesn't care

He never did exercise, and just never would
But ran to the trough as fast as he could
He was ever so greedy, and I'm sure you'll believe
He's first to the trough, and last one to leave

The trough was the length from his tail to his nose
And roughly as deep from his teeth to his toes
It was almost as wide as Dougies big tummy
And filled with the food that Dougie thought yummy

But one day young Dougie was feeling quite rough
He just didn't think that he'd eaten enough
So he did something selfish and ever so mean
He climbed in the trough to lick it all clean.

Though Dougie was horribly dirty and smelly
He stood in the trough; then lay on his belly
He felt really happy as he licked the trough clean
He's the greediest piggy that I've ever seen.

He finally came to the end of his dinner
He'd got a bit fatter; for certain not thinner
Because he'd been greedy he'd run out of luck
When he tried to stand up he found he was stuck.

He shifted and squirmed as he tried to get out
But Dougie was stuck from his tail to his snout
He started to worry. He started to squeal
"If I cannot escape I'll miss my next meal".

The pigs gathered round to see why the din
"Oh dear" said one of the pigs with a grin
"What miserable luck" said Doug looking sad
"Could one of you please fetch my mum or my dad?"

"You shouldn't be greedy" said a pig looking stern
"And you need to eat less. I think you will learn"
"We'll all try and help, but we'll probably fail"
"As there's nothing to grab but your ears and your tail"

They pushed and they jiggled and tried a quick nudge
But Dougie was stuck and just wouldn't budge
"We could pull with a rope" said one of the mums
But it wouldn't have worked. They hadn't got thumbs

The noise then attracted the Donkey and Duck
Very surprised to see Dougie was stuck.
They laughed at poor Doug getting stuck in the trough
Which was hard for the Donkey as he had a cough.

COUGH
COUGH
COUGH

The chickens, the goats,
the geese, and the bunny,
All came to see what they found quite so funny.
The famers' cat Puddles came out of the house,
This was more fun than chasing a mouse

"Were you trying to find
somewhere different to sit?"
"Or just being greedy
or being a twit?"
"I was hungry" said Dougie,
"and just didn't think."
"Now I'm covered in food
and starting to stink."

"We'll fetch the farmer. He'll know what to do,"
"Though he'll take a few pictures, and laugh a lot too."
So they made lots of noise to grab his attention
And knocked on the door with some apprehension.

Though looking quite fuzzy, out came the farmer
He was covered in hair from shaving the llama
"The llama's half shaved. He looks like a poodle"
"How'd you get stuck in the trough you great noodle?"

So he pulled Dougie's ears, and then pulled his tail
Then wobbled and jiggled him to no avail
A pig jammed so firmly is tricky to shift
"I could tip you out – if I get help to lift"

So he gathered some help, as Doug weighed a tonne
The postman, the farmhand, his brother, and son
They tipped it right over with a squelch and a slurp
But it just didn't work, and made Dougie burp.

The farmer was thinking, then scratched his bald head "I'll have to find something to pull you instead"

He thought for a minute, then shouted, "of course! I'll get a big rope and Donald the Horse".

Dougie was holding the rope in his teeth
As they couldn't quite get the rope tied underneath
It was tied to the horse - like when ploughing a field
And then pulled to see if young Dougie would yield.

Dougie was holding the rope really tight
And Donald was pulling with all of his might
His legs were now shaking and started to buckle
A wobbly old horse made the goat really chuckle.

The horse couldn't shift him, of that there's no doubt
And Dougie was scared that his teeth would fall out
So the horse gave up pulling - from the struggle so brief
And no teeth were missing to Dougies relief.

Farmer then said after lengthy deduction
"The only way out is a belly reduction"
"You may end up stuck for a week at this rate"
"You'll only escape when you lose lots of weight"

They'd all given up. There seemed little hope
They'd tried lots of things like the horse with the rope
But then something happened, really quite unexpected
As Dougie was feeling quite sad and dejected.

"Oh no" said young Dougie. "That's just what I feared"
As Brian the naughtiest Turkey appeared
The most badly behaved of all on the farm
His appearance was always a cause for alarm.

He's usually the cause of the trouble that's seen
Like when somebody painted the sheep blue and green
When bunny escaped and rode on the goose
And of course, the day that the turkeys got loose.

But Brian did nothing, which was a surprise
He just stared at Dougie with curious eyes
He looked at his tail, and looked at his snout
Thinking of ways to get Dougie out.

He stood for a while, and did something clever
He tickled the end of his snout with a feather
Dougie just giggled as without a doubt
The tickliest part of a pig is his snout.

It started to fizz at the end of his nose
Then shot down his legs and into his toes
It shot through his tail and up to his eyes
Then in both his ears - which was a surprise.

It went round his belly and back to his knees
Dougie was building an enormous sneeze
He couldn't control it. He just couldn't stop
As he sneezed and shot out from the trough with a plop.

He rolled and he bounced, and fell on his back
He knocked over the duck, who gave a loud quack
He landed on donkey, who wasn't too pleased
He'd been eating his breakfast when Dougie had sneezed.

The goat laughed again, unkind I suppose
As donkey had carrot stuck right up his nose
He sneezed - it shot out - and knocked over Duck
Who was having five minutes of really bad luck.

"I'm off back to bed" said Duck with a quack
As Dougie now lay in the yard on his back
"When will I learn" said Doug in a pickle
As Brian then gave his big tummy a tickle.

"Now that will teach you to share with the others
Your sisters; your friends; and all of your brothers
So, don't be so greedy, just have your fair share"
Said farmer who gave him his grumpiest stare.

From then on young Dougie had tried to eat less
Which wasn't too easy he had to confess
He now waits his turn, and tries to be fair
But climb in the trough? Well - he just wouldn't dare.

The End

Also available in

The Wobblebottom Farm Series

Have you been to Wobblebottom Farm?

If you've walked by the stream; crossed the bridge by the trees
Past the whispering willow as it sways in the breeze
Crossed Buttercup meadow, to honeypot lane
To Saint Andrew's church with its gold weathervane

Turned left at the church yard to Rumbletum Brook
A nice place to rest on the bench with a book
Did you sit watching swans swimming regally by?
And gaze at the swallows as they soar through the sky?

Did you walk down the riverbank, over the stile?
And followed the path for a tenth of a mile?
Through a hole in the hedge where the corns growing high
And looked for the place where the field meets the sky?

Did you see the old house, all surrounded by flowers?
A beautiful site, you could gaze at for hours
Did you feel it could welcome you into its arms?
As one of old England's most beautiful farms

...then you probably asked the daft donkey for directions to
Wobblebottom farm – and he's sent you to the wrong place!
That's Honeydew Farm – where his brother lives.

Made in United States
Troutdale, OR
12/16/2023

15965369R00021